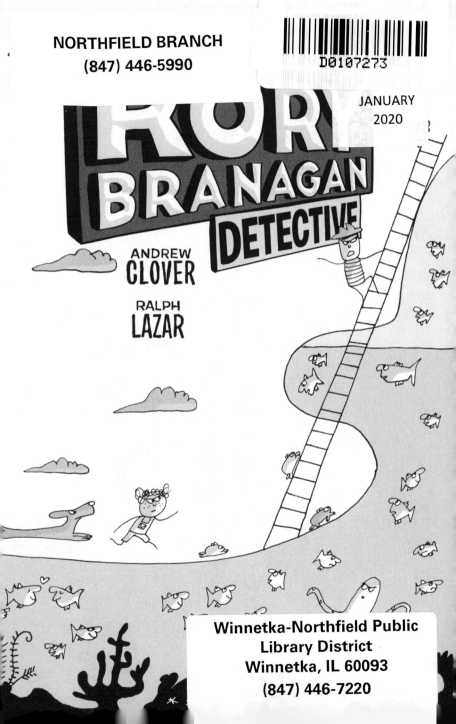

RORY
BRANAGAN
DETECTIVE

ANDREW
CLOVER

RALPH
LAZAR

RORY BRANAGAN
(DETECTIVE)

CASSIDY CALLAGHAN

WILKINS WELKIN

SIOBHAN BRANAGAN

PADDER BRANAGAN

SEAMUS BRANAGAN

AUNTIE JO

STEPHEN MAYSMITH

MRS. WELKIN

ANDREW
CLOVER

RALPH
LAZAR

RORY
BRANAGAN
DETECTIVE

Penguin Workshop

W

PENGUIN WORKSHOP
An Imprint of Penguin Random House LLC, New York

Text copyright © 2018 by Andrew Clover.
Illustrations copyright © 2018 by Ralph Lazar. All rights reserved.
First published in Great Britain in 2018 by
HarperCollins Children's Books.
Published in the United States in 2020 by Penguin Workshop,
an imprint of Penguin Random House LLC, New York.
PENGUIN and PENGUIN WORKSHOP
are trademarks of Penguin Books Ltd,
and the W colophon is a registered trademark of
Penguin Random House LLC. Printed in the USA.

Visit us online at www.penguinrandomhouse.com.

Library of Congress Control Number: 2019033122

ISBN 9781524793647   10 9 8 7 6 5 4 3 2 1

To all children who love a laugh,
to all those who love *adventure*,
to all those who see *bad guys* and *deadly danger*
and who are not afraid to *keep going*,
we dedicate this tale.
Keep *fighting*, friends, keep fighting.
Be bold, be curious, be DETECTIVES!!

I am Rory Branagan. I am actually a detective.

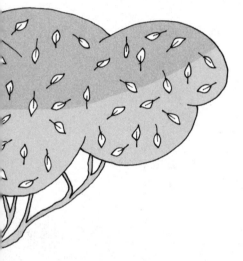

This is my tree house den. It's where I come to read, relax, and *spy on people*.

That is my mom.

That is my brother.

That is Mrs. Welkin, my neighbor,

and—**yes!**—

I *detect* that she is with . . .

Wilkins Welkin,

her dog,

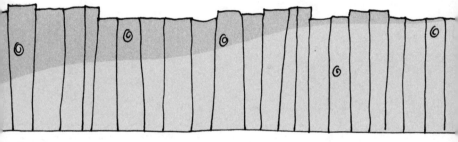

who is probably my best friend in
the whole world!!

You might think it's a bit weird having

a best friend who's a sausage dog.

But Wilkins comes over most afternoons
and usually we go out and mess around
with balls in the park.

He's just like a normal best friend.

The only difference is . . .

. . . he'd never come around on a bike.

And if we're
watching TV,
he only *really*
pays attention . . .

. . . if there's a cat on the screen.

He even comes for sleepovers, and I don't mind admitting that when he does Wilkins Welkin and I . . .

. . . we do hug.

As he *dreams* he kicks his little sausage
legs, and just *thinking* what Wilkins might
be dreaming about makes me smile.

I basically have an amazing life.

But . . . there is just one bad thing
about it, which makes me worry at night,
and that is . . .

NO ONE TELLS ME ANYTHING!

They don't.

And the thing they definitely don't tell me about is the thing I *most want to know*, which is . . .

Why did my dad disappear when I was three?

He did.

One moment he was there in the park, pushing me on the swings so hard I felt I was flying like Superman.

And the next . . .

He was gone.

Why did he go?

And where did he go?

Those two questions are always
swirling like fish in my head.

Those two questions are always there.

Well . . . those, and . . .

It was my tenth birthday last week.

I was thinking: *Does my dad even KNOW?*

I was thinking: *Does my dad even CARE?*

I was thinking . . .

But finding out
what happened to
Dad—that's what
turned me into
a detective.
I'll tell you the
whole story . . .

CHAPTER ONE
It All Starts

On a Tuesday, 5:22 p.m. . . .

I am walking home, and I am in a
REALLY GOOD mood, because I have
been at Corner Boy Gilligan's house.

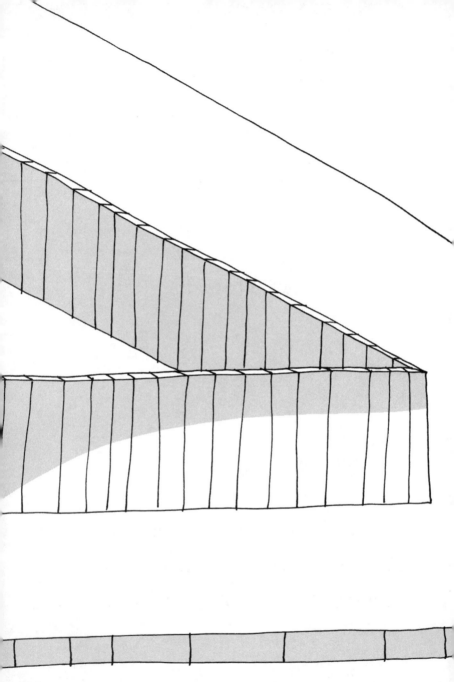

His real name is Connor, but we call him Corner Boy, because he is always standing on the street corner trying to look fierce. Literally, he has a spear, and if you go near him without asking, he hits you.

But I actually like him. He also has forty-two guinea pigs, and I am allowed to play with them whenever I want.

Today the Gilligans had loads of

blender boxes . . . and we made a gigantic

GUINEA PIG
OLYMPIC STADIUM.

It was hilarious.

We scattered carrots up and down the track, and the guinea pigs were going wild.

They were *sprinting* around squeaking
for joy. We made them race.

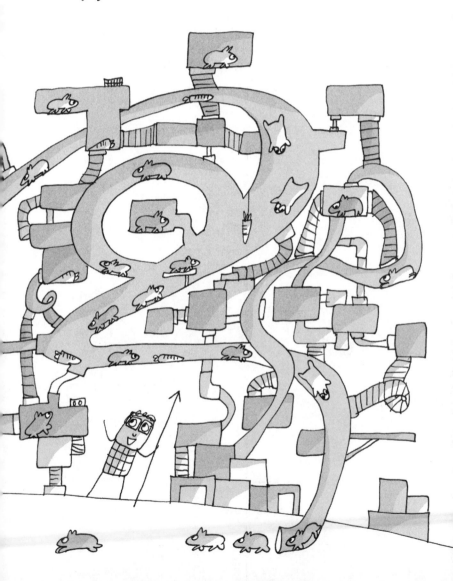

We even gave out medals made from cucumber.

We gave most of them to Mike Tyson. He is our favorite guinea pig by a mile. He is the HUGEST, the FASTEST, and the GREEDIEST.

If he sees food, he charges like a hippo,
and he smashes the others out of the way.

We gave him ten medals, which he ate.

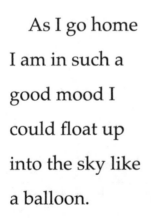

As I go home
I am in such a
good mood I
could float up
into the sky like
a balloon.

As I enter the house

I even find a letter for me.

I am going to take it upstairs,

to read it.

But then, as I'm *going up the stairs*, I overhear my mom *jabber-wabbering* away to my Auntie Jo in the kitchen.

She's saying, "So I said I'll MEET you, but NOT at my house . . . and HE said . . ."

Right away it felt like when you're out swimming and the water goes cold.

I am thinking: *Who is she meeting? Is it Dad?*

I go back down.

...So I said I'll MEET you, but NOT at my house...and HE said...

But as soon as I go into the kitchen,
they are as silent as statues.

They are as silent as statues

that are

deep,

deep

below the sea.

I say, "Mom, what is happening?"

She's suddenly very interested in the dishes. "Mrs. Welkin is coming over," she says. "She wants to play Boggle."

"But who are you seeing?" I ask. "Are you seeing Dad?"

"RORY!" says Mom (very loud). "I need to speak to your Auntie Jo!"

Then she puts on her being-nice-to-Rory voice. "Go upstairs and see your brother. He *wants* to see you," she says, and she *shoos* me out of the room.

I am thinking: *It is very, very, very, very unlikely my brother wants to see me.* But if I go in his room, it will wind him up.

So I go.

My brother's name is Seamus. His
room is dark and stinky like a cave.

But it's here that I first see someone
very, very important.

. . . and do I

slide down

till I find a

huge puffer

fish that has

hair like Donald Trump, who says

"I will tell you what happened to your

father, young man"?

NO! (That would be deranged!)

What *happens* is, I go in and I smell a smell like a hundred dead fish all being sick at once . . .

And I see my brother.

He is sitting on the bed glaring at me over his trading cards, like a *crab* that's looking out over a rock. "What do you want?" he says.

"Well," I say. "*I would LIKE to know . . .
WHERE Mom is going, and IF she is seeing
Dad, and IF we even have a dad.* And I
would also like to know . . ."

At this point I look out the window.

"*Who* is moving in next door?"

Right away I am *drowning* in curiosity.

The house next door has been empty for three whole years. It has been one of the biggest mysteries on the block.

Who would buy a house, then not use it?

House next door

I am about to find out.

my house

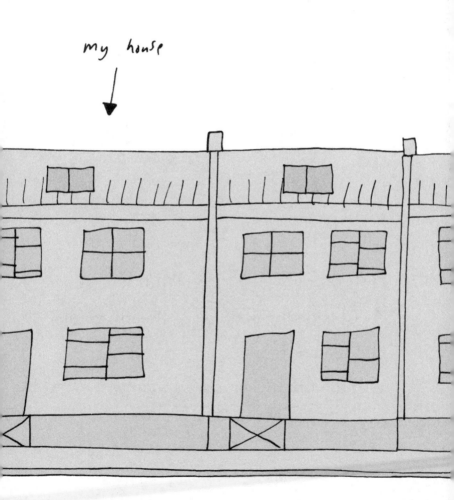

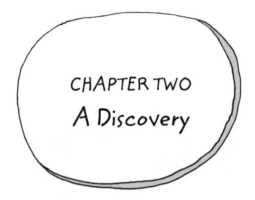

CHAPTER TWO
A Discovery

I hurry down to the street. But when I
get outside the people are already going
into the house.

In the front room I see a man with
boxes.

In the bedroom upstairs I see a woman with blonde hair that's floating around her head like cotton candy.

I peek through their front door. I see . . .

. . . a girl.

She's carrying boxes to a room at the
back. She's about my height, and I so
want to know what her face looks like.

"Mom," I say, running through to the kitchen. "A family is moving in next door!"

"What are they like?"

"I'm finding out," I tell her, heading out into the garden.

I put my eye to my special peephole in the fence.

"I can see them!" I call.

"What is the mom like?" calls my mom.

"She is probably the most gorgeous mom in the world!"

"After me!"

"After you, Mom!"

"And what about the dad?"

"He does not seem to go with the mom at all!" I say.

"Why not?" says a voice.

I turn. I now notice something I might have noticed earlier but I didn't (because the peephole doesn't let you see much at once) . . .

The girl is not in the back room. She is in the back garden wearing a cool blue hat. She is looking right at me while eating a lollipop.

"Hello!"

she says.

"I'm

Cassidy

Corrigan."

"I'm Rory Branagan," I manage to reply.

Then she just *looks* at me.

And I realize she is probably the *best-looking* girl I've ever seen, and she is *definitely* the most CONFIDENT, and it makes me feel a little *dizzy* as if I've just rolled downhill.

"Do you live here?" she asks.

"Yes!"

"Which is your room?" she says.

"That one," I say (pointing).

"I'll be just on the other side of that wall," she says.

I say nothing.

I can't think of a single question to ask
her, and I realize I should think of one fast,
because I am staring at her like an idiot.
But then suddenly I think of loads of
things to ask.

"Where have you just moved from?" I say.

"Oh," she says. "The other side of town."

"But which part?" I say.

"Oh," she says. "You wouldn't know it!"

I say: "Don't you start doing it, too!"

She says: "WHAT?"

"NO ONE TELLS ME ANYTHING!" I shout. "And it drives me *nuts!*"

Cassidy Corrigan comes so close I can see her freckles through the peephole.

"Tell me," she says. "What do you most *want* to know?"

"I'd like to know WHERE my dad went," I tell her. "He disappeared when I was three. And I'd just like someone to tell me WHY."

She comes so close I can see the speckles in her eyes and smell the lollipop on her breath.

"You know what you should do," she whispers.

"What?" I say.

"You should become a detective," she says, "and you should FIND OUT, and I, my friend, *will be your Sidekick.*"

I say: "What's a Sidekick?"

"It's a helper," she says. "Like Sherlock has Watson, and Superman has Lois Lane."

"But," I say. "Will I be Superman?"

"You won't *be* Superman," she says.

"You'll just be Rory Branagan (detective) and I'll help."

I am already thinking: *I like this!* I will be like some kind of Super-Detective, who flies round the world solving crimes.

But I figure, if I'm going to be a detective, I should play it cool. "Well, I suppose I could give it a try!" I say (quite modestly).

"Boomtown!" she says.

And then, to my astonishment, she just LEAPS over the fence.

I cannot believe how easily she does it.

"How did you do that?" I ask.

"Ah," she says. "That's nothing."

And then she plonks her hat on my head, turns toward the house, and stalks straight in like a fox.

CHAPTER THREE
Cassidy Starts Making Mayhem

"Hello, Mrs. Branagan," says Cassidy, as she *sweeps* past my mother in the kitchen. "I'm the new neighbor!"

My mom stops me as I scuttle past like a little lobster.

"What are you doing?" she says.

"I am just showing her around,
Mother!" I tell her.

"Well, don't you *dare* go into my room,"
she says.

"I'm not that stupid!" I tell her.

And I'm not. I mean . . . my mom is great. She is *really* great. But if she catches you doing anything bad—for example, fighting or going into her room—she turns into an evil witch, and she does not

stop shouting till you've shrunk down to the size of a worm.

"Don't worry," I tell her. "I will NOT go into your room!"

I turn and run
after Cassidy.
She's already
halfway up
the stairs.

"Don't go into the room on the right,"
I tell her (catching up with her).

"Why?" she asks.

"That's my brother's . . . Go in there
and he'll *rip* your head off!"

"Sounds *exciting*!" she says (her eyes
gleaming).

She goes right in like a policeman
making a bust.

"I'm Cassidy Callaghan," she says.

"Pleased to make your acquaintance."

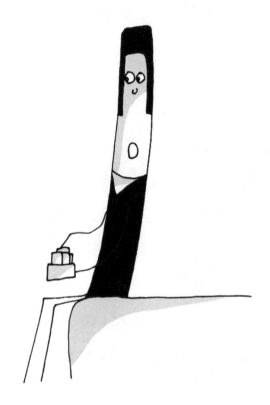

My brother stares at Cassidy like an idiot.

He could not have been more surprised if a unicorn (that was tap dancing and singing the songs of Justin Bieber) had come in.

It's actually embarrassing.

I have to pull her out of there. And only when I've got her in the hallway do I say it.

"You just said you were Cassidy Callaghan," I whisper.

"And?"

"*Outside* you said you were Cassidy Corrigan."

"I didn't," she says, blinking her eyes like a cat. And she turns.

I see she's going toward my room.

Oh.

Oh no . . .

I am suddenly
wishing my room
was about
four hundred
times better.

I'm
wishing
it had a
swimming
pool, and
maybe a
spaceship.

77

I'm wishing it had a mirror that leads
to another land.

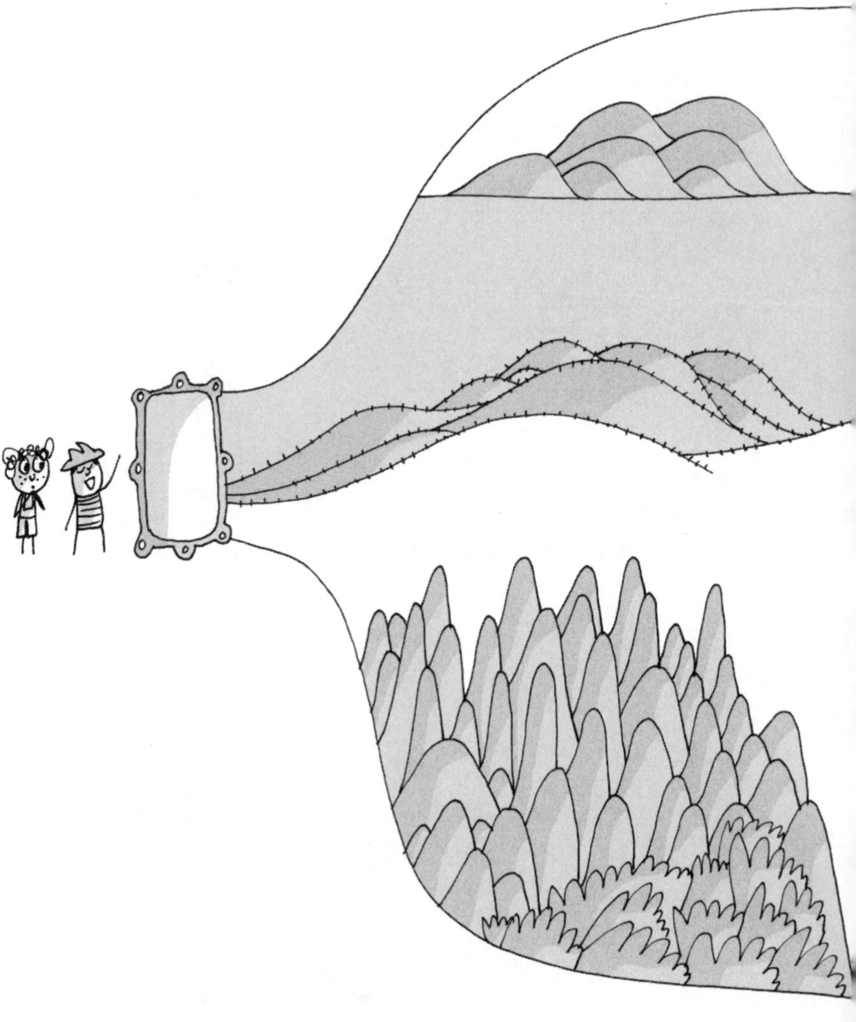

79

But, in fact, my room is small, and dark, and it smells of cheese. It's like the room of a mouse.

I like it. I have a picture of Dele Alli on the wall (my favorite soccer player). I like that. But I can tell Cassidy is not impressed.

"Oh," she says.

She leaves.

Next she heads up the stairs.

"Who lives up here?" she whispers.

"My Auntie Jo," I tell her. "Well, she's not my real aunt. She's just a friend who rents the room in our attic."

"So," she says. "Are you coming?"

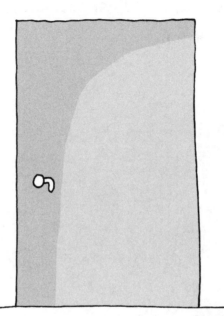

I don't feel good about going into Jo's
room, but Cassidy is waiting for me.

"Oh yes," I say. "I'm coming."

I stride past her and go in.

I've been in here loads of times.
My brother and I watched all of
Sherlock with Jo.

And *Stranger Things.*

And *CSI*.

We've spent loads of time with Jo in here.

But she's not here now.

In fact, her room is weirdly empty.
There's just a pile of leaflets on the
bedside table for the Deadly Pirate,
the new restaurant where she's started
working. I take one.

Cassidy is still standing in the doorway.

"How long has she lived here?" she says.

"Two years."

"And did you clear the room out before she came?"

"Yes!"

"Then there won't be any evidence of your dad here," she says. "Not unless he's hiding in the attic—like a big rat."

"Ratman!" I say.

I like the idea of this!

Ratman!

He climbs up the drainpipes.

He steals your cheese.

I open the door to the attic.

I look around. Cassidy has *gone*. Oh no.

I catch up with her outside my mom's room.

"I don't think you should go in there!" I whisper. "I'd definitely *feel bad* about you doing that."

"Listen, young man," says Cassidy, raising her finger, "if you want to be a detective like Sherlock Holmes, you must *Master Your Emotions and Investigate the Facts!*"

Then she goes straight into my mom's room.

I so want to go in too. But, if Mom catches me in here, she will definitely go full witch. But if I don't go in, I may never find Dad.

Should I go in?

I go in.

I enter to find Cassidy rooting through the closet.

"So how long is it since your dad disappeared?" she whispers.

"Seven years," I tell her.

"Well, your mom seems to be keeping his clothes," she says. She hands me a pair of jeans.

"And what did he look like?" she says, now moving to a chest of drawers.

"Tall, dark hair," I say.

"Sort of like that?" she says. And she pulls a photo out of a drawer.

I see a picture of my mom. She's with my dad. He is handsome and kind looking, and he's standing by a car. Right away, I recognize him.

I also recognize the car. I haven't seen it since Dad disappeared and that seems important, but I don't know why.

It's as if the memory is buried deep, deep underwater and I would need to swim down past big, evil creatures to find it.

But I so want to find that memory in my mind.

But then the
door opens and my
brother's BIG HEAD
appears. You can tell
he's very bothered
we're in Mom's room.

"What are you doing?"
he says.

"Just . . . being a detective!"
I say.

"Why would YOU ever be a
detective?" he says.
"You're a dork!"

And I can't think
of anything to say to
that, so I don't.

I just stuff the jeans on his head.

Cassidy laughs. And he just runs out, furious.

BOOMTOWN!
RESULT!

Then suddenly we hear my mom on the stairs. I get the *fear*. We both get the *fear*, and we leg it out of there. It takes us 0.2 seconds, and we're out and the door is shut by the time my mom gets there, but *somehow*—I don't know how (I think that all moms *are* actually half witch) . . .

. . . she still knows we've been in her room.

"You need to go home now," she says
to Cassidy in a voice that is so calm it is
actually creepy. Then she turns to me.
"And, Rory, Mrs. Welkin is coming soon.
You need to clean up your art project in
the living room."

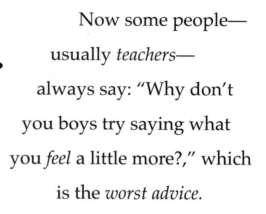

Now some people—usually *teachers*—always say: "Why don't you boys try saying what you *feel* a little more?," which is the *worst advice.*

What I *want* to say is: I have told you a HUNDRED TIMES that I *will* clean up the art project in the living room.

Or I could say: "Mom, why do you have a picture of Dad that you never show me? I have told you a THOUSAND TIMES I want you to *show me things!*"

I could easily say that.

But then my mom could so easily say:

"And I have told you **one** million times *not* to go into my room!!"

And then the people on the other side
of town will see my mother *burst through
the roof* as she turns into the *biggest, evilest
witch IN THE WORLD!*

And I do not need that.

The world does not need that.

So on behalf of the world I suck it up
and keep quiet.

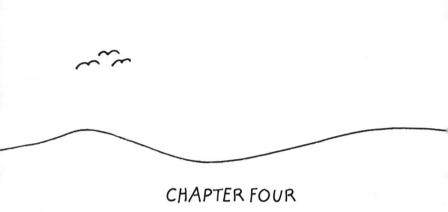

CHAPTER FOUR
I Suck It Up

I go to the living room, where, if I had to talk about my feelings, I'd say I feel bad.

Even though it was a little scary, I was enjoying showing Cassidy around, and I'm *ANNOYED* my mom's made her go home. And as I look around at the mess, and I see that most of it is actually *my brother's*, I feel worse.

I notice I'm still holding the leaflet for the Deadly Pirate.

There is a picture of the front of the restaurant. It looks like a ship.

I am thinking: *I wish it was a ship . . .*

I'd sail it far, far away . . .

I'd sail past islands . . .

I'd sail so far off there'd be big whales

leaping from the waves . . .

. . . then I think: *Even if I could sail so far that the farthest-flying seabirds couldn't reach me . . .*

. . . *I know that — SOMEHOW — my way would still be blocked by . . .*

... the **big head of my brother**.

Then I am thinking: *What would I actually do, if my way was blocked by the giant head of my brother?*

And I am thinking . . . *I would sail my ship right up his nose!!!*

And then
I am having
a grand old
time, thinking
how funny it
would be,
if I could sail an
actual ship into
the head of
my brother,
when
suddenly
I realize that . . .

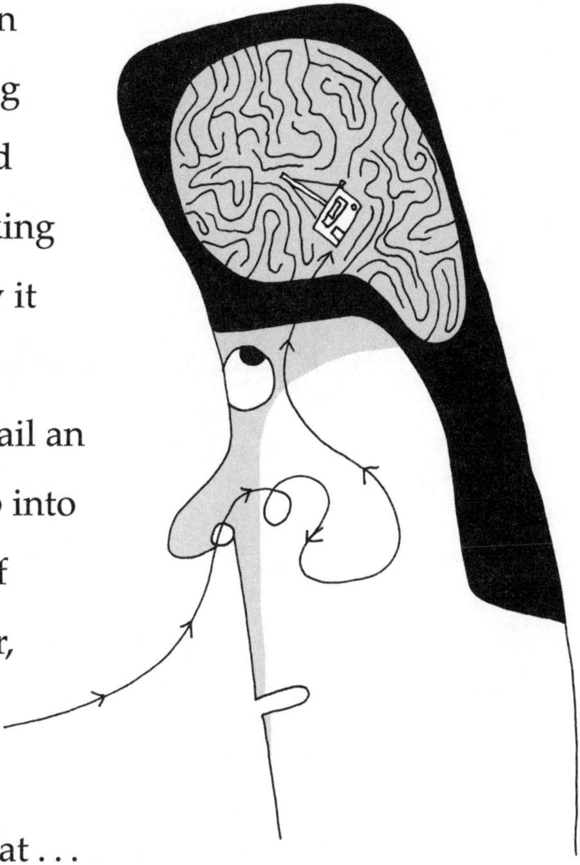

in the REAL world ...

Auntie Jo has come in.

"Did you go into my room?" she says.

"No!" I tell her.

"I know you're lying!" she says, and
she smiles.

"How?" I say.

"Because you closed your eyes," she
says. "Like this . . ."

And she closes
her eyes slowly.

"It's a classic sign
of lying!" she says.

I'm thinking:
She's right! And I
am also thinking:
*And where else did I
see someone do that
today?* I'm trying to remember.
It seems important.

"Plus," says Jo, "you are holding my
leaflet in your hand."

"Oh," I say. "I'm sorry."

"Ah, don't worry," she says. "You're all right with me! Just don't do it again!"

She gives me a gorgeous smile, then she heads off to work.

And if I were a real detective, I would probably be thinking, as I watch her walking past the front window: *Why was her room so empty?* But I'm not. I am thinking: *Ah, and you're all right with me, Jo!*

I am thinking: *If I did have a ship that could sail far, far across the sea . . . you could come.*

But then I stop thinking about boats and Jo. I even stop thinking: *Why is there a picture of my dad that my mom's never shown me?*

Because right then I notice something very interesting out the window . . .

*

CHAPTER FIVE
An Actual Crime

⟶

First of all, I see . . .

Corner Boy who is standing on his corner.

He looks around. Then I look around.

And we see . . . arriving, with a swish
of tires, a mysterious car. It's a silver
Mercedes-Benz. It has blacked-out
windows. *Whose is that?* I am thinking.
Then . . .

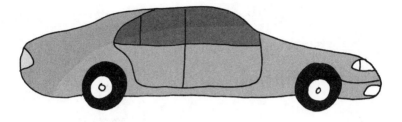

As I watch, Corner Boy's dad gets out holding a box of take-out food. His real name is Graham Gilligan. But we call him Guinea Pig Gilligan, because he is the one who breeds all the guinea pigs.

Everyone knows Guinea Pig Gilligan, who is about the friendliest man on our block. Every evening you'll hear a knock, and you'll open the door to find Guinea Pig with a big smile on his face and a

blender, or a George
Foreman Grill, that
he's offering to sell for
almost no money at
all.

But the
friendly man
is not smiling
now.

As I watch,
he takes a forkful of his food. And
then suddenly he freezes. And then he
bends right over, and he starts going
honnnnnnnnk honnnnnnnnnk
like a donkey.

Why is he doing that?

Right away I am *very bothered* and *very interested*. I need to know what's going on, and I run toward the front door.

But then suddenly my
brother appears (because my
brother always appears when
I am trying to do something).

"WHAT are you doing?"
he says.

"Something is wrong with
Guinea Pig!" I tell him.

"So," says my brother. "Why
are YOU going out there?"

"Because I need to know what's
going on!"

"Rory, you're NOT a detective!"

This is annoying me.

"What will you give me," I say, *"if* I PROVE
I am a detective?"

"I would give you," he says, "*my complete collection* of trading cards from the years 2010 to 2018, but I would never do that, because you are *not a detective*!"

"Well," I shout to him, "I will *prove* to you that I am!"

"How are you *supposed* to do that, you *big bumhead*?" he says.

"For a start," I tell him, "I will *find out* what's happened to Corner Boy's dad!"

And I pull open the door.

And I go over to investigate.

Guinea Pig Gilligan is still doubled
over, but he now staggers to his front
door all stiff. He goes in. Corner Boy tries
to follow. His mom appears. She pushes
Corner Boy out.

I then appear.

"Corner Boy," I say, walking up his
path. "What happened to your dad?"

When Corner Boy sees me coming to
help, something comes over him.

He punches me and I go down.

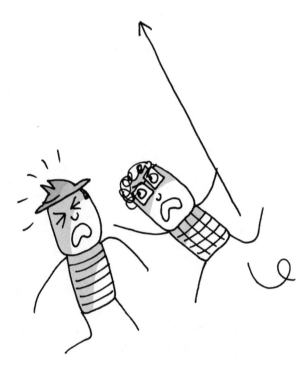

"Corner Boy!" I say. "Why did you
DO THAT?"

"I'm sorry!" he says. "I have a medical condition that makes me hit people!"

I don't *believe* there's a medical condition that makes you hit people.

But I don't say that. I get to my feet.

And when I get up I see Corner Boy
is trying not to cry. He's not doing well.
He's staring into the distance, and his
bottom lip has gone
all quivery.

I hate it when people cry. I don't think
I could be a detective, if people cry.

But then someone else arrives.

Hallelujah!!

It's Cassidy. She'll know what to do. For some reason she's standing up on her front wall.

"Cassidy," I call. "This is my friend Corner Boy!"

"Hello!" she says.

He looks at her, all confused.

She beams at him. "I'm Cassidy Callaghan," she says (leaping off the wall and swaggering over). "I am pleased to make your acquaintance."

She smiles and holds out her hand to
shake.

Now, we're not used to shaking
hands on our block, and, seeing Cassidy
advance like that, Corner Boy *panics*.

He dodges Cassidy's hand.

Then he tries to whack her.

 But it's as if
she's expecting it.
She ducks,
and then, using
the speed of his
whack, she just
casually swings
Corner Boy around . . . and then she
neatly *judoes him down*.

One second later,
she's pinning Corner
Boy to the ground.

"I'm *sorry*!" he says. "You just *scared* me!"

"It's fine!" she says. "But don't do it
again!"

"I won't!" he says.

"Good!" says Cassidy, and then, totally
cool, she pulls him up. "You threw a nice
punch, by the way."

She pats him on the back, while winking at me over his shoulder.

"How come you're so good at fighting?" I whisper to her.

"Ah . . . You just have to think what the other person is about to do," she says.

"Then you **surprise** them."

CHAPTER SIX
Cassidy Starts Her Investigation

"But are you OK?" Cassidy asks Corner Boy.

I look into his face and see one big tear
that's ready to burst out.

"My dad has just collapsed!" he says
(sounding a little squeaky).

"What happened?" Cassidy asks.

"I don't know!" he says. "He was just eating his take-out food, then he collapsed. I think someone might have POISONED him!"

"But who would want to poison him?" she says.

"I don't *know*!" he says.

"But why might they?"

"Well, I am not saying he would," says

Corner Boy, "but some people might think my dad might want to speak to the police."

For a moment Cassidy's eyes flash.

"How come your dad might want to speak to the police?" she asks.

Just then there's a loud *vroom-vroom* and a police car arrives.

It stops.

Then a shiny shoe steps out of the car, followed by the biggest man we've ever seen. Corner Boy actually runs off. I just stand there, and moments later, he's looming over me, as big as a whale.

"Who are you?" I ask.

"I am Stephen Maysmith," he says, "police detective!"

"Wow! Have you come to investigate the poisoning of Guinea Pig Gilligan?" I ask. "I'll help you!"

"Er . . . no," says Maysmith. "I am just here to have a routine chat!"

And he waves a package of cookies at me.

"He won't be eating those!" I say. "I think he's been *poisoned*!"

Right then the door opens behind me. It's Corner Boy's mom.

"Of course he hasn't been poisoned, officer!" she says. "He's fine! He's in the living room!"

She smiles at Maysmith and gives us an evil look.

Then she shuts the door with a bang.

"Is he in the living room?" asks Cassidy.

"I'll look!" I say, and I pin my eye to the mail slot.

"What can you see?" she says.

"More than you'd expect," I tell her (glad I've got some information at last). "Normally this hallway is filled up with blender boxes, but Corner Boy and I had to burn them."

"What?" says Cassidy. "How come you had to burn them?"

"His mom said she didn't want the mess!" I say. "We made a Guinea Pig Olympic Stadium. But the only part left is the medal podium. I'll ask Corner Boy to show you!"

"Corner Boy!" I shout.

He appears at the garden gate.

"I don't think you should shout," he says.

"Why?"

"My dad has collapsed!" he whispers.

"Yes," I tell him, "but your mom says he's fine now!"

"Yes," says Corner Boy. "But I don't think he is."

"Oh," I say (feeling serious all over again).

"And the worst thing is . . . ," says Corner Boy (sounding very squeaky indeed), "Mike Tyson has escaped!"

Corner Boy seems more bothered by the loss of Mike Tyson than the collapse of his dad.

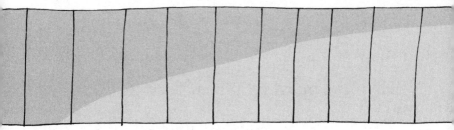

He goes still. And I can tell why. He's wondering what could have happened to Mike Tyson, and suddenly he works it out. We both do. We both run. Right away we're both fearing what we might find, and we're both right.

Mike Tyson is lying on his side.

He has food near his mouth. His eyes are shut. He actually looks *dead*.

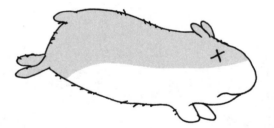

And now Corner Boy can't help himself.

He picks up Mike Tyson. Then he *bursts* into tears and runs *screaming* into the house. He slams the door.

As it shuts with a BANG I turn to Cassidy, who's totally cool. It's as if this is what she *expected* to happen.

"*Interesting,*" she says. "*Very, very interesting.*"

"What's *happened*?" I say.

"Well, I don't know for sure," she says.

"But it *looks* as if the dad was selling a whole load of stolen goods, including *blenders*—probably on behalf of a gang. Then the police want to talk to him, so your man Guinea Pig has tried to *destroy* the *evidence* by burning the boxes. But the gang was still worried that Guinea Pig might squeal, so they *poisoned* him."

As I am looking at her, the questions are swirling in my head like fish.

I am thinking . . .

Is Guinea Pig a thief?

I am thinking . . .

I am thinking . . .

I thought *I* was supposed to be the detective. She just worked out about ten detective things in four seconds flat.

"How did you work all that out?" I ask.

"Oh," she says. "Well . . . the whole family has got a *suspicious* amount of money. (I mean . . . look at the new car.) And then the mom is obviously trying to hide something from the police . . . (*Why? What's she hiding?*) Those are the main clues."

I just look at her with astonishment.

She is now peering at a box on the floor.

"And then of course there is that!" she says.

I look.

There's a skull
and crossbones
on the box.

"Do you
think that's a
message,"
I say, "from
the poisoner?"

"No," she says. "I think that's printed
on all the boxes."

"Yes," I say. "But where have those
boxes come from?"

"I don't know!" she says, turning again.

"Because I think they're from the Deadly Pirate," I say.

"Ah . . . I think it came from a real person," she says, "not a pirate."

"It's a restaurant," I tell her, and to prove it to her I get out the leaflet. "I think we should go there *right now*. And find out who put the poison in Guinea Pig's food!"

"I'm not sure about that," she says.

"If there is poison in that restaurant,"

I tell her very fiercely, "then I also need to warn my Auntie Jo because she *works* there!"

She looks into my eyes.

"I think we should go back to your house," she says, "and investigate your dad."

"I thought that *I was the detective*," I growl, "and *you were the Sidekick*."

She looks back at me a long time.

Then suddenly . . .

"All right, boy!" she says, smiling.
"You're on!"

And we go.

CHAPTER SEVEN
The Trip into Town

"Where is this place?" she says as we head off.

"It's on Main Street!"

"Isn't that miles away?"

"Don't worry!" I tell her. "I know some shortcuts."

"Like what?" she says.

"Like *this*," I say, and I *dive* through a break in the fence.

We come to a bank that is very steep but it has a whole load of sandy earth on it.

"And this is how you get down this," I tell her.

And I just surf down.

At the bottom there's a ravine with a river. There's also a rope swing.

"I'll show you how to do this," I say, and I swing.

You have to come flying off at the end . . .

. . . then you have to leap like a squirrel to the top of the bank, and you have to grab one of the tree roots . . . then you pull yourself up.

Cassidy is watching me and luckily
I do it perfectly.

But in the end
she just swings
her own way.

First she climbs
up the tree to make
the swing longer.

Then she flies down . . .

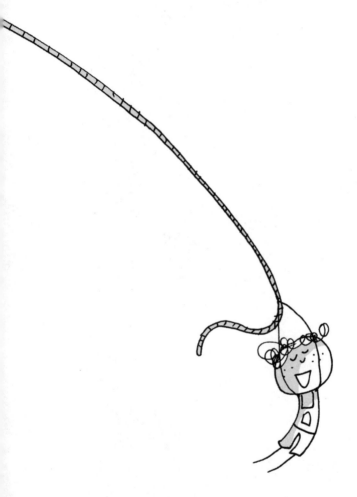

. . . and at the end, she springs off
(way higher than I did) . . .

. . . and then finally she leaps like a cat to the top of the bank.

After that we're right outside the
Deadly Pirate.

Looking through one of their round porthole windows, I can actually see Auntie Jo. I like how she let me off for going into her room. I am glad I am going to rescue her.

"I'll do the talking," I tell Cassidy, and I stride over.

As I open the door to the Deadly Pirate, I am thinking: *This is about the coolest place I've ever seen*. It has wooden stairs, like on a ship. The walls are decorated with swords and lanterns and rusted pirate stuff.

I go up.

At the top of the stairs I see a fish tank. There is a light and bubbles and a castle, and outside that a tiny octopus is sitting, looking like an old lady on a bench.

In the restaurant, Auntie Jo is facing me. As I arrive, for 0.26 seconds, her eyes are blank. Then . . . she beams. "Rory Branagan!" she says.

Then she crouches and whispers in my ear, "What are you doing here?"

I lean close to her ear. "Someone has been poisoned," I whisper. "In this restaurant."

"Who?" she says.

"Guinea Pig Gilligan."

She smiles. "Is that a person?" she asks. "Or a guinea pig?"

"What is going on?" says
a voice behind me.

And I now turn and
see a very shady-looking
person.

Well . . . I'm not
a real detective yet,
and so I cannot point
at people saying "That is
definitely the criminal!"
But this man's got a
stubbly face and angry
eyes, and he looks like Dracula.

"This restaurant," I say (approaching),
"has given out some food that has
poisoned my friend's dad."

"Who?" says Dracula.

"Guinea Pig Gilligan,"
I say, and . . .

Even Dracula laughs.
And his laugh is a
very Dracula type laugh.
"Uh-huh-huh!"

"Is that a *real person*?"
he says. "Or a cartoon?"

"It's a REAL
PERSON!" I shout.
"I am *telling* you . . .
there is a *poisoner*
here, and we
need to find out
who it is!'

They are laughing even more.

I am not liking this at all. When I
became a detective I did not expect to be
laughed at by everyone. *Where the heck is
my Sidekick?*

I look out of the round porthole
window, and I now see that Cassidy
hasn't even come in. *What?!!* I am in here
all alone, and meanwhile she is outside

rooting through the trash cans like a little fox.

"Does your mother know you're here?" says a voice.

Oh no! I turn and see Mrs. Daniels. She is the lady from the school office whose main job is to give you an evil look when you're late for school.

Now she's sitting here, about to eat some soup.

"I wouldn't eat that," I tell her. "It could be *poisoned*."

"Thank you," she says. "I shall make up my own mind about that," and before I can stop her she takes a big slurp.

She then smiles. It's an evil, sarcastic smile and she's got a bit of spinach on her teeth, and for a second she looks all deadly like a big jellyfish.

I just run out.

I find my Sidekick still out by the trash cans.

"Did you tell your aunt?" she says.

"Yes!" I tell her.

"And what did she do?"

"Laughed. They all laughed."

"If you're going to be a detective," says Cassidy, "they're going to try to stop you in loads of ways, and laughing won't be the worst."

"But do you think they're poisoning people?" I ask.

"Well," she says. "These boxes do have the skull and crossbones. But I couldn't know for sure that someone inside is a poisoner unless I saw where they're getting the poison from, or if I could see them putting it in the food."

"But where would they actually do that?" I ask.

"Probably the kitchen."

"But how would you get to the kitchen?"

"I don't know," says Cassidy

 Callaghan, shrugging. "But if it were me, I'd go down that alleyway."

She points.

I turn.

CHAPTER EIGHT
The Alleyway

There is a dark alleyway along the side
of the restaurant.

At the end there's a wooden door that
stops you from going into the little yard
behind the restaurant. As we look down

the alleyway we hear a strange shriek,
like an animal being hurt. Then the door
at the end opens, and a man appears.

He's a round man with a big belly that
is peeping out of the front of his shirt like
an eye. He comes waddling toward us.
He's holding a garbage bag, and trying to
listen to his phone.

He's right over us before he actually
sees us.

"What are you guys doing?" he says.

"We think that Guinea Pig Gilligan was
poisoned," Cassidy tells him, looking at
him carefully. "We're trying to find out
who did it."

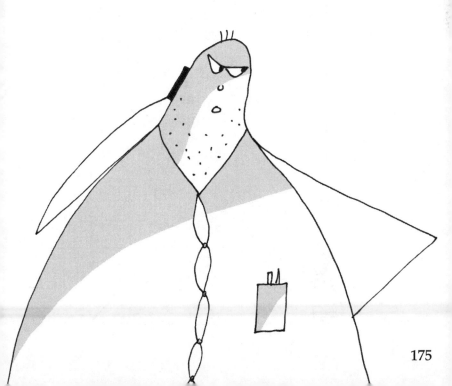

"Well, I'm not surprised," says Belly Man. "Guinea Pig must be the biggest thief in town! At some point *someone* was going to put a stop to it!"

He puts the garbage bag down by a lamppost and turns away.

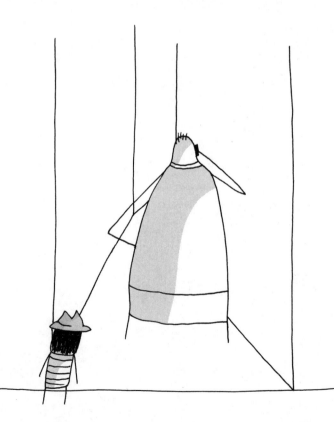

I go after him.

"Who would put a stop to Guinea Pig Gilligan?" I ask.

"There're basically two people, aren't there?" he says.

"Who?" I say.

He *really* doesn't want me asking him.

It's obvious I'm annoying him, but I am already thinking this is something that might make me special as a detective: I don't mind being annoying. I have a brother; I spend my days being annoying.

And as the man tries to go I think: *You can turn away and head off into the darkness like a big fish. But I will follow you, like the little line of poop that is always trailing behind the fish's bottom.*

I almost knock into the man as he
stops to unlock the door at the end of the
alleyway.

"What do you want?" he says.

"I want to know," I say, "who are the two
people who might put an end to a thief."

"Well . . . the first is Michael Mulligan,"
he says.

"Who's that?"

"He's basically the biggest crime lord in the land," he says.

As I look back up at him I am imagining Michael Mulligan . . .

MICHAEL MULLIGAN

The Biggest Crime Lord in the Land

Huge as a mountain, he has a hundred homes on each shoulder.

"And who's the other person?" I ask.

"The other person is Jack 'Muscle' Thompson. You do crime in this town, you answer to Jack 'Muscle' Thompson, and if he thinks you might talk to the police, you get SHUT DOWN." And he

gives me a fierce look, as if just the name
Jack "Muscle" might scare my very soul.

But the trouble is I am not imagining
Jack "Muscle" Thompson.

I am imagining . . . Jack Russell
Thompson.

He's a gangster, but he's also a little dog.

He breaks into your house, and
bites your postman.

He beats up your cushions.

And if he really wants to annoy you,
he drags his bottom on
the carpet, like a dog
with worms.

I'm so busy imagining Jack Russell, that Belly Man goes off and shuts the door.

Then there's a smell, like one hundred dead fish all being sick at once, and my

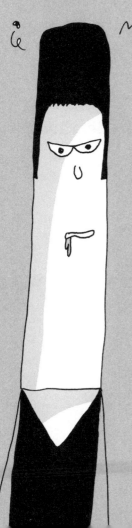

brother's BIG EVIL FACE comes looming out of the darkness. He's eating a fish stick all slathered in ketchup.

"What are you doing?" he says.

"Just being a detective," I tell him.

"You are not a detective," he says.

"And you're also not allowed to go into town. I *am*, because I am thirteen, but you . . ."

Right away he is being so annoying.

Cassidy walks off ahead of us.

I then have to walk all the way home, being followed by my brother, who is saying, "Face it, you are not a detective!"

He is being so annoying.

Then, even when we have reached our home, and Cassidy has been driven off into her own house, my brother is still saying: "Face it, Rory, you are NOT A DETECTIVE!" and then he shoves his fish stick in my face, and . . . I know that Cassidy has told me, if I want to be a detective, I must *Master My Emotions and Investigate the Facts* like Sherlock Holmes, but Sherlock Holmes was never hit in the face by a wet fish stick, so I suddenly lose it, and I try to JUMP KICK my brother.

But I miss. I always miss. And I end up with my brother sitting on me as if I'm a chair.

"Face it," he says. "You're not a detective!"

"GET OFF ME!" I shout.

I'm just thinking this could not get any worse, but then my mom appears, and right away she screams,

"Why *are* you two fighting?"

My mom has gone full witch. But luckily my brother gets off me. He then goes inside. And luckily my mom goes inside too. She bangs the door shut.

So then I'm just standing out on the street, trying not to cry.

And I am all alone—except for Corner Boy. (He is also standing, as per normal, out in the street.) Even *Corner Boy* is sorry for me.

"You OK?" he says.

If I speak, I know I'll cry. I just nod.

"My mom just called an ambulance," he says.

I say: "Good."

But I still don't dare look into Corner Boy's eyes. I just stare at his sneakers. They're new ones.

He comes walking over. I can tell he wants to talk.

"But I don't know why someone would do that to my dad!" says Corner Boy.

I look at him. I look at the hoodie he's wearing. It's a new one, an expensive kind.

"Corner Boy," I say, "I think your dad might be a thief!"

"He is *not!*" shouts Corner Boy. He's immediately very angry. He thrusts his spear at me. (I don't mind. I just catch it!) And then he runs off crying.

"Corner Boy," I shout. "Don't you
even want your spear?"

I go after him, offering up his spear.
I try to give it to him.

Corner Boy turns. "KEEP IT!" he
shouts, and he pushes the spear back at
me so hard I fall over.

Unfortunately that's when my mom
comes out.

"Rory!!!
Have I not
told you **a**
MILLION
TIMES
that you are not to fight
in the street? Right!
You can go to your room!
What were you doing?
WHAT were you doing?"

"I am just being a detective,"
I tell her.

"You are not a detective, and you will **NEVER** be a detective

EVER

AGAIN!!!"

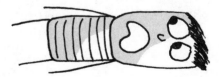

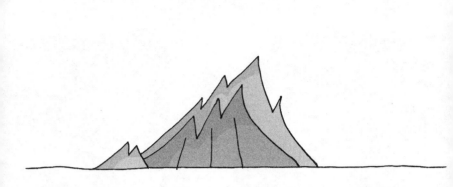

CHAPTER NINE
In a Deep, Dark Hole
Under My Brother

One minute later, I am in my room.

And I am feeling like a tiny, shivery
worm that is right down the deepest,
darkest hole, trying not to cry.

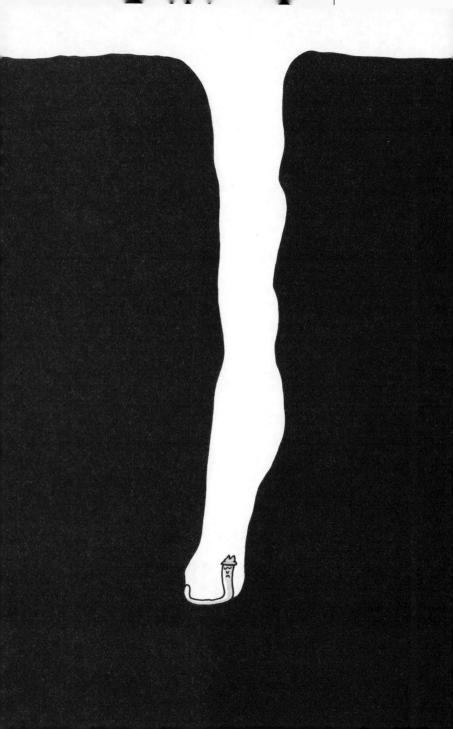

There's a knock on the window.

Cassidy's face appears.

"You have to go," I tell her. "If my mom finds me being a detective again, she'll kill me."

Right then my mom appears.

Luckily Cassidy has disappeared in time. I look up at my mom. I am hoping she has come because she wants to show me that she's not mad anymore. But then I look at her face, and I see she still is.

"I am still angry," she says (as if I didn't know), "that you tried to kick your brother, which is extremely stupid, and dangerous. I am going out in five minutes. I want you to go and apologize to him."

Once she's said that she goes.

So now I have to
go and apologize to
my brother, which
is my worst thing in
the entire world.

So now I'm
feeling like a tiny,
shivery worm that's
at the bottom of the
deepest hole, and
who has just been
bitten by a snake.

I am feeling *paralyzed*. I feel so bad.
I am actually feeling like Corner Boy's
dad must have when he'd just eaten the
poisoned food! I feel I can't *move*.

But I *make myself move*. I go to my
brother's room.

As I walk in, I feel about as big as a
shrimp.

"Seamie," I say.

He says nothing. I can tell I am going to cry and so I need to speak fast.

"I am sorry," I say, "that I tried to kick you."

My brother gives me a look that is actually not that evil.

"It's OK," he says. "I know you're bothered about Dad and sometimes it gets to you."

I say nothing. I always expect my brother to be horrible, and now that he is being nice I find it SO CONFUSING, and now I'm definitely in danger of crying. I can feel the lump in my throat.

"You've just got to face it," says my brother. "Dad was a great dad, and we loved him. But he isn't coming back, and that's all there is to it."

And I wish he hadn't said that. As soon as he does the tears just come *pouring* out of my eyes, and I can't stop them. They just roll down my face, and I cry. I cry loads. Soon there'll be so many tears I could be swimming in them.

I am thinking of last summer. Corner Boy's dad had one of those long inflatable mats. He squirted water, then he slid down it like a crazy beetle on its back. And now I'm thinking: *I actually like Corner Boy's dad*—who is about the only dad on our block—*and I definitely do not want him to die*, and I cry more.

And then I think of Mike Tyson the guinea pig. He didn't mean anyone any harm (unless they were eating his vegetables) and now he's been POISONED, and I definitely don't want him to die either for something that wasn't even his *fault*, and I cry even more.

But . . . one good thing about my brother: if I'm crying, he doesn't try to stop me. He lets me cry. I cry. (I actually start to *enjoy* it.) But suddenly I've had enough . . . I open my eyes, and I see my brother, who has been waiting for me to finish. He wants to say something. "Did you hear?" he says.

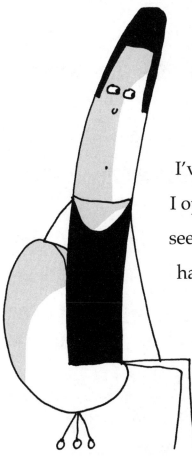

"Jo persuaded Mom to meet that man at the Deadly Pirate. I would *not go* there. Craig Hairfield went last week, and he said they have a blue-ringed octopus, which is about the most *lethal* animal in the sea."

"I have seen that octopus," I say. "It is about as big as a lemon, and about as scary."

"Wellllll . . . ," says my brother, and as he reaches around to his computer, for a moment he looks like a blue-ringed octopus, and I can't help but smile. I'm like that when I've been crying. My emotions are everywhere! I could easily start *laughing* now. My brother moves

his fingers
like tentacles.

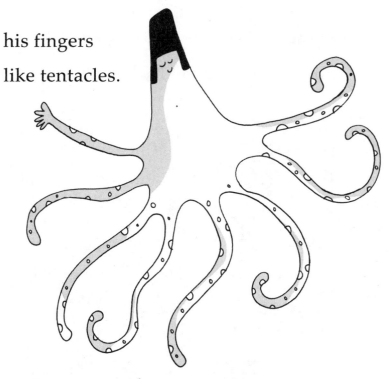

"Let me see," he says, and I am
definitely starting to feel a laugh filling
my chest like a bubble.

And just then I look out the window. I
can see Mom is leaving and Mrs. Welkin
is arriving. I can see she's brought Boggle.

I can also see she's brought Wilkins Welkin.

I can see he's brought his hedgehog.

And it's hard to feel too bad when you're about to be visited by a sausage dog.

But my brother doesn't even notice them coming. That's why *I'm* a detective and he isn't. He doesn't *notice* anything.

He starts reading out facts from his computer.

"The blue-ringed octopus," reads my brother (with evil pleasure), "has a store of tetrodotoxin behind its salivary gland—where it has enough poison to kill twenty-eight people."

I go cold.

"Upon contact with the poison," continues my brother, "the victims first lose all liquid around their mouths, then they go stiff, then they get paralyzed, then they *die*."

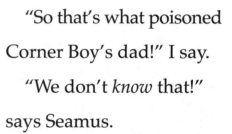

"So that's what poisoned
Corner Boy's dad!" I say.

"We don't *know* that!"
says Seamus.

"We *do*!" I tell him. "And we definitely
do not want Mom eating at that restaurant!
We have to keep her from going!"

"Rory," says my brother, "you cannot

let Mom find you being a detective again.
I swear she may actually just bite your
head clean off."

"Well, that's a risk I'm going to have to
take," I tell him, "if I'm *going to save her
life*! At the very least I have to warn Mom
of the danger."

"She will kill you," says my brother.

"She won't *literally* kill me," I say. "But if she eats poison, she might *literally* die."

My mind is now made up. I am thinking: *I am definitely scared of crime lords and poisoners, I am now scared of*

the blue-ringed octopus, and I most definitely
am scared of my mom, and I definitely don't
want to upset her again.

But more than that I want to get at the
truth of what's happened.

I feel *it doesn't matter if the truth is a long, long way off and it's on the other side of cold, stormy seas.*

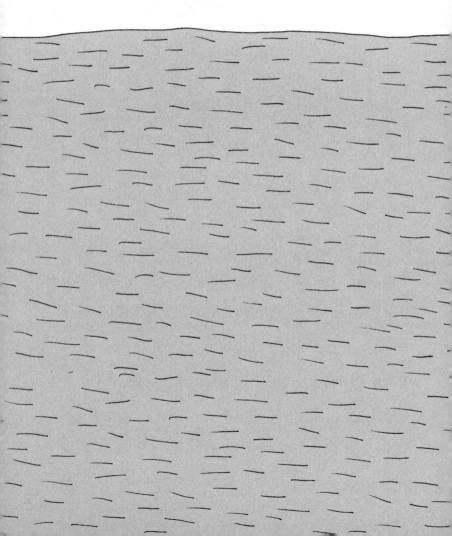

I must get to it.

"You can't *stop* me," I tell my brother. "I need to warn Mom."

"No," says my brother. "You need to play Boggle with Mrs. Welkin."

"No, *you* need to play Boggle with Mrs. Welkin!"

"I'll go now," says my brother, "and I'll tell Mrs. Welkin you'll be *right down*, ready to play Boggle."

"You do that!" I answer. And he does.

And I immediately climb out my window toward Cassidy. I tell her everything.

"Give it five minutes," I say. "Then knock, loud. Say you need me."

"All right, Mr. Detective!" she says. "I will!"

217

CHAPTER TEN
Reinforcements Arrive.
And We Go Out to Beat the
Bejesus Out of the Baddies

Five minutes later, I am playing Boggle
with Mrs. Welkin.

I'm also with Wilkins.

I swear he thinks he's a detective too!
He is standing with his feet up on the

sofa, and he's looking out, growling, as if he's heard a rumor that there are some *bad* cats out there, and he wants to get them.

Suddenly there's a huge banging on the door. It's as if we've been attacked by a pack of wolves.

"Rory!" shouts a voice.

"Sorry about this," I say to Mrs. Welkin.

As I open the door, I see a last burst of
evening light beaming into the hallway.
I also see Cassidy Callaghan, and she is
smiling like a cat.

"Are you ready?" she says.

"Wait," I say.

I put on the hat she gave me earlier. I also put on the coat my mom bought me last week. It suddenly seems a whole lot cooler.

"You look *deadly*!" says Cassidy, smiling more. "In fact, I am going to call you Deadly Branagan!"

"And you look like a big cat," I tell her. "I am going to call you Cassidy 'the Cat' Callaghan!"

"I like it!" she says.

Just then Wilkins arrives, and right away he goes to the front door. He pokes his nose outside, sniffing for cats.

"Mrs. Welkin," I shout, "I am just going next door to my friend's for one or two hours!"

"All right, dear!" she calls.

"Can I take Wilkins?" I ask. (She knows I love Wilkins!)

"All right," she calls.

And I am very pleased about that.

And the moment we step out onto the street all the streetlights come on together, and just for a moment I feel as if . . . I have my coat, my hat, my Sidekick, and also a brave dog who thinks he's a detective, and I feel that . . .

I am Deadly Branagan, and I am ready for anything.

As we go down the road an ambulance is outside Corner Boy's house. Stephen Maysmith is standing around the back, as if he's waiting for fish and chips.

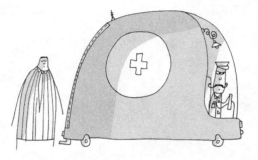

"I found out that Mr. Gilligan might have eaten food that had tetrodotoxin in it," I tell him. Then I say it again, so the ambulance men will definitely hear. "*Tetrodotoxin*," I say.

"Thank you," says Mr. Maysmith. "I wouldn't worry yourself. We also found out he may have eaten nuts to which, we believe, he was allergic."

"Did you hear that?" I say to Cassidy.

"They thought that Guinea Pig had been poisoned by nuts. So telling them about the tetrodotoxin could maybe have saved his life."

She just prowls onward.

"And this could save ours," I say. And I pick up Corner Boy's spear.

As we stride off down the street I can't help but smile.

"What are you smiling about?" asks my Sidekick.

"That finally I feel like we're getting to

the bottom of things," I tell her.

"Do you?" she says.

"Oh yes!" I tell her. "I feel like we're getting to the bottom of the bottom."

"And when we get to the bottom of the bottom," says the Cat, "do you think we'll find a poop?"

"Well, if we do," I say, "we'll take it home and give it to my brother." We both laugh.

5.6 minutes later, we're outside the Deadly Pirate.

We tie Wilkins to the lamppost. He immediately turns and sniffs. There is something down that alleyway that bothers him.

I am crouching by the trash cans. But in my head I am making a diagram of EVERYTHING THAT I KNOW about what might lie ahead.

Meanwhile Cassidy scampers out into the middle of the road, checks the restaurant, then comes back.

"I saw your mom," she says. "She is with a man."

"Who?" I ask.

"I couldn't see him very well," she says. "But let's go in." She heads toward the front.

"But *wait*," I tell her. "I don't think you should just walk in like that. Because it would be best if I could see first, who my mom is actually with, and what she's talking about."

"Good thinking," says Cassidy. "So how will we get in?"

"Like this!" I say. And I turn and
sprint off down the alleyway.

At the end the wooden door to
the yard is shut.

But I don't care about that.

I spring onto the door handle and then
leap right over, like Cassidy.

For a moment I am **Rory Branagan,
Super-Detective**, and I'm flying in to
the rescue!

The next moment I smack the ground
(which is a lot farther down than I was
expecting).

I am
actually
quite
winded.

Meanwhile Cassidy just walks through the door, all casual.

"You OK?" she asks.

"Yes!" I tell her. "Except for the big pig."

There actually is a big pig. He comes waddling toward me.

"Why would they keep a pig in the back?" I ask.

"To eat the scraps," says the Cat. "Also to eat anyone who tries to come in the back."

I leap out.

I go over to the Cat, who now is by the back door of the kitchen.

We peek inside. I see Belly Man from the alleyway. He is scraping food off plates with his fingers. In the kitchen, there's Dracula. He's standing by a man who's chopping something. This guy has a knife and a huge hairy eyebrow like a caterpillar.

Just then Auntie Jo comes into the kitchen. We run back outside.

"So which one of them is the crime lord?" I whisper.

"Oh," she says, "a man like that has someone else to do his dirty work. That's why you'll never catch a crime lord."

"How do you know?"

"It's obvious," she says. "But someone here is working for the crime lord. They're the one who has done the poisoning. They're still the murderer. And we have to work out which of the four suspects did it."

I am thinking of all four suspects.

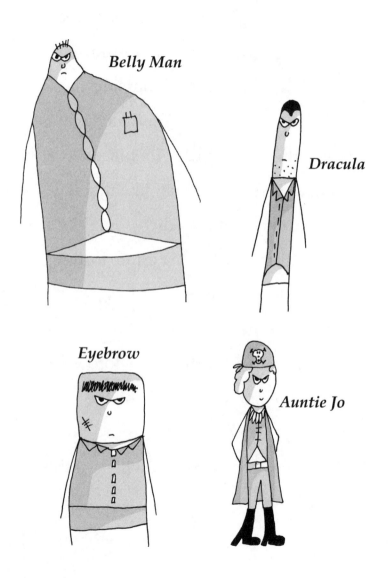

Belly Man

Dracula

Eyebrow

Auntie Jo

Now the questions are swirling in my head once again, but now they're all asking the same thing. I'm thinking . . .

"I think it's Belly Man from the alleyway," I say.

"But he is only cleaning the plates," she says. "So he's not in the best place to put in the poison."

"So then it's the one who looks like Dracula," I say.

"Why?"

"I just don't like him."

"*Master Your Emotions*," she tells me, "*and Investigate the Facts*."

"Who do you think it is?" I ask.

"I think it's your Auntie Jo," says Cassidy.

I say nothing. Even thinking it might
be Jo makes me feel like I'm drowning in
dark slimy water that's filled with snakes
and confusing questions.

I am thinking . . .

But she is my friend . . . could she be a POISONER?

I'm thinking . . .

*Her room was WEIRDLY EMPTY. Is she about
to
RUN?*

I'm thinking . . .

*So why hasn't she gone? (Is there something she
wants
to do FIRST?)*

Then I'm thinking: *I need to get inside.*

"It could be two people working together," says Cassidy. "This is what we must find out."

Suddenly I am *so scared*. But she smiles.

"So," she says (eyes gleaming). "Shall we go in?"

I do not want to go in. But just then Belly Man appears at the back door, holding a bucket.

We go as silent as statues.

We're also as silent as statues at the
bottom of the sea.

Belly Man has now gone past. Cassidy then grins at me, as if to say: *this is our chance*. And I can feel my heart bump-bump-bumping.

I count: one, two, three . . . I am about to go in.

"You coming?" says Cassidy.

"Try stopping me!" I say.

And, together, we enter the scene of the crime.

CHAPTER ELEVEN
Entering the Scene of the Crime

We both float through the first room.
When we reach the kitchen the only
person there is Eyebrow, chopping. For a
moment it looks as if we might be able to
float right by him.

But then Dracula appears.

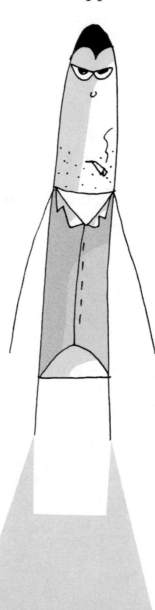

We both duck behind the fridge.

Dracula talks quietly to Eyebrow. We just

stay stock-still, and as we do, the questions are swirling in my head like sharks.

I am thinking . . .

And . . .

And . . .

But how would you even GET POISON from an OCTOPUS?

And a moment later I get my answers.
From here we can see into the restaurant.
I can't see Mom yet, but I can see the
tank.

Just then Jo steps toward it. She holds
a skewer of food out to the octopus.

Suddenly his rings go dark, and he attacks the skewer, and you can tell he's biting it with **lethal poison**.

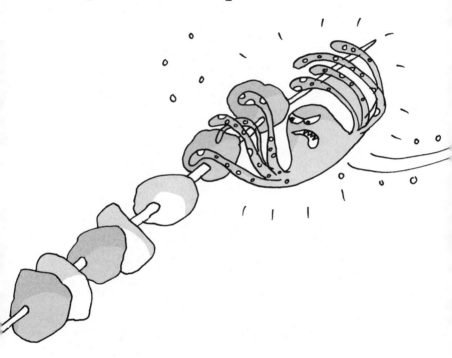

Meanwhile, I am just looking at Auntie Jo. She is completely still. Her eyes are totally cold.

And as I look at her I am completely still as well.

First I am shocked.

Then I am paralyzed
(as if my insides
were filled
with stinging
jellyfish).

Then I am as cold as a detective standing on the thick ice of the North Pole, and I think:

Oh my God, that is not my Auntie Jo.
That is a stone-cold killer, who needs to be
put in prison.

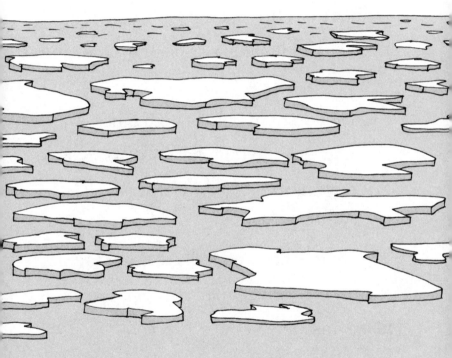

But then I see that she's walking toward us. We dodge back behind the fridge.

She gives the poisoned meat to Eyebrow. He has two other skewers in front of him. He starts adding the poisoned meat to one of them.

Then he and Jo stare at each other, and only now do I think: *Whose food is it that they are wanting to poison? Could it be Mom's?*

Auntie Jo turns and places the empty skewer carefully in the trash can. Eyebrow places his knife in the trash can.

For about 0.48 seconds they are both turned away.

In that moment I see there are now two

skewers with meat. I see that one could be Mom's. I don't want ANYONE to be poisoned, but most of all I need to save Mom. *But which is her plate?*

One of them is piled high with spinach, which my mom loves. That must be her plate. It's *the one with the poisoned skewer.* I switch the skewers around.

Just then Jo starts to turn. Cassidy and I both duck down totally silently and leave.

We have gotten through the kitchen without anyone noticing us.

In the restaurant we squat down
beside a big plant.

As I peer around it, I see Mom. (She's
all dressed up with lots of makeup,
which makes me feel a little sick.)

Through the plant I see Mrs. Daniels,
who is now tucking into her pudding.

But who is Mom talking to? I peek
around the plant again. I see . . .

Stephen Maysmith the police detective!!

He is looking at her with a big smile smeared over his big cheesy face. I do not like the way he is looking at her.

But what are they talking about?

"And this is Michael Mulligan," says Maysmith, and he passes over a picture, of a fierce man with a beard.

"Do you know him?" asks Maysmith.

"No," says Mom, and she shuts her eyes.

What? I'm thinking. *Is she lying? Does she know Mulligan?*

"And this is Jack 'Muscle' Thompson," says Maysmith.

"Why would I know a person like that?" asks Mom.

"We know Thompson has people working and living in this area," says Maysmith.

He looks at Mom.

I look at Jo. She's hovering with the
skewers, looking white.

"And how about this?" says Maysmith,
passing over another picture.

It's my dad!

"Well, that's my husband," says Mom.

"Yes," says the detective. "Where do
you think he is?"

The questions are definitely swirling
like sharks now.

I'm thinking . . .

Yes! Where IS Dad?

I'm thinking . . .

But WHY does Maysmith
want to know?

I'm thinking . . .

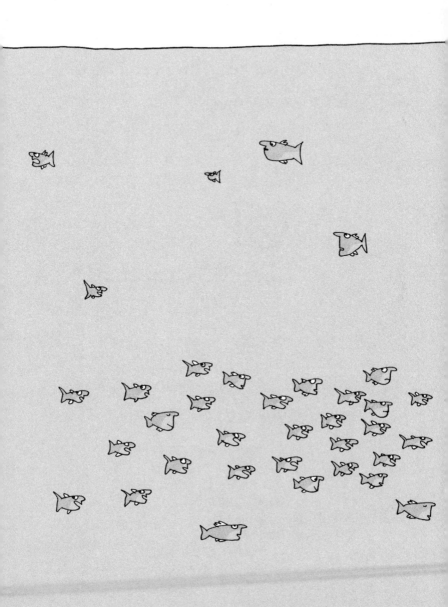

But Mom says nothing, and just then Jo steps forward and serves the food.

My mom lifts her skewer, and I see it's the poisoned one.

"NO!" I shout.
"Do NOT eat that!"

My mom can't believe I'm here.

Nor can Jo.

"Rory!" says Mom.

"It's poisoned!" I say.

"Don't be ridiculous!" she says.

"It's the same stuff that poisoned
Guinea Pig Gilligan!"

"It certainly doesn't look poisoned," says
Mom. "And it costs fourteen ninety-five."

My mom hates waste. She'd almost
rather be poisoned than waste fourteen
ninety-five.

I look at Jo.

I'm thinking: *Does she know she's given
Mom the poisoned skewer?* I'm thinking:

*Is that what she
wants?*

But I can't wait
to find out. Mom
is about to eat.
I spring into action.

CHAPTER TWELVE
Action.
Fast, Lethal Action

I leap forward and *fwap* the skewer
off Mom's plate. It flips through the air,
landing in front of Mrs. Daniels.

She leaps to her feet. Maysmith stands
too.

His chair hits Mrs. Daniels in the back of the legs.

She goes down like a tree being chopped.

Her hair falls in the candle, and goes up like a torch.

I grab a glass of water and splash it— direct hit—on her head.

I think I got the flames the first time, but I take no chances. I grab the water jug, and dash the whole thing right over Mrs. Daniels's hair.

S
 p
  l
   a
    s
     h.

(It feels good!)

"What are you doing, you crazy fool!"shouts Maysmith.

He grabs me, but I wriggle away like an eel.

"It's not me you want!" I shout, pointing at Auntie Jo and Eyebrow, who are watching from the kitchen. "It's them! *She* is the one who decides who to get, then she tells him, and he *poisons* them."

"But why would Jo want to poison me?" says Mom.

"It's him they want!" I shout, pointing at Maysmith. "*He* knows Muscle Thompson has people working here. And *I* know Jo's done the poisoning, and that's why she's about to leave."

"What do you mean?" says Mom, looking at Jo.

"Everything in her room's packed," I tell her. "She's off."

Mom turns toward Jo. Jo just edges toward the kitchen. So does Eyebrow.

"Quick!" I shout. "AFTER THEM!"

Maysmith is way too slow. The bad guys are far too fast for him.

But they're not fast enough for the Cat, who leaps like a tiger through the hatch.

She pushes a serving cart into Eyebrow.
He pushes it back.

She grabs a huge frying pan. She leaps
onto the cart, she surges across the room
like a knight riding in and then . . .

BAM!

She conks Eyebrow with the pan.

Eyebrow is down. He is on the floor like a fish.

But Jo is still going. She chucks a can
at the Cat.

The Cat grabs a trash can lid and
smashes the can aside.

Jo grabs the lid, then smacks the Cat
with it and runs!!

I cannot believe it.

This is a woman who's made me smoothies a hundred times. Now she's whacking girls on the head with trash can lids. What will she do next?

Suddenly I see it . . .

And I know what I'm going to do.

Jo turns and sprints for the back of the restaurant.

The Cat flings plates at her. Jo bangs them off with her shield.

She gets through the yard door.

And that's where she's stopped by
Wilkins Welkin, the dog detective,
who comes **CHARGING** in.

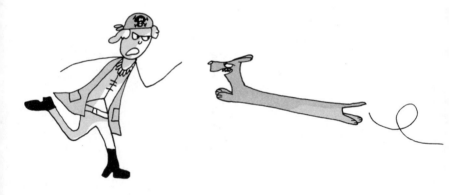

(To be fair, it's not her he's after.
It's the pig. But he does enough to trip Jo
and stop her for two seconds.)

And then I COME

ROARING IN

WITH THE SPEAR!!!!!

But the trouble is Jo sees me coming.

She bashes down the spear, and she

yanks and pushes, and before I know it

I'm *pole-vaulting* over the door. Then Jo is

free and alone!

Except for my mom.

Who takes her out with a cutting board.

No one messes with my mom.

(Well done, Mom!)

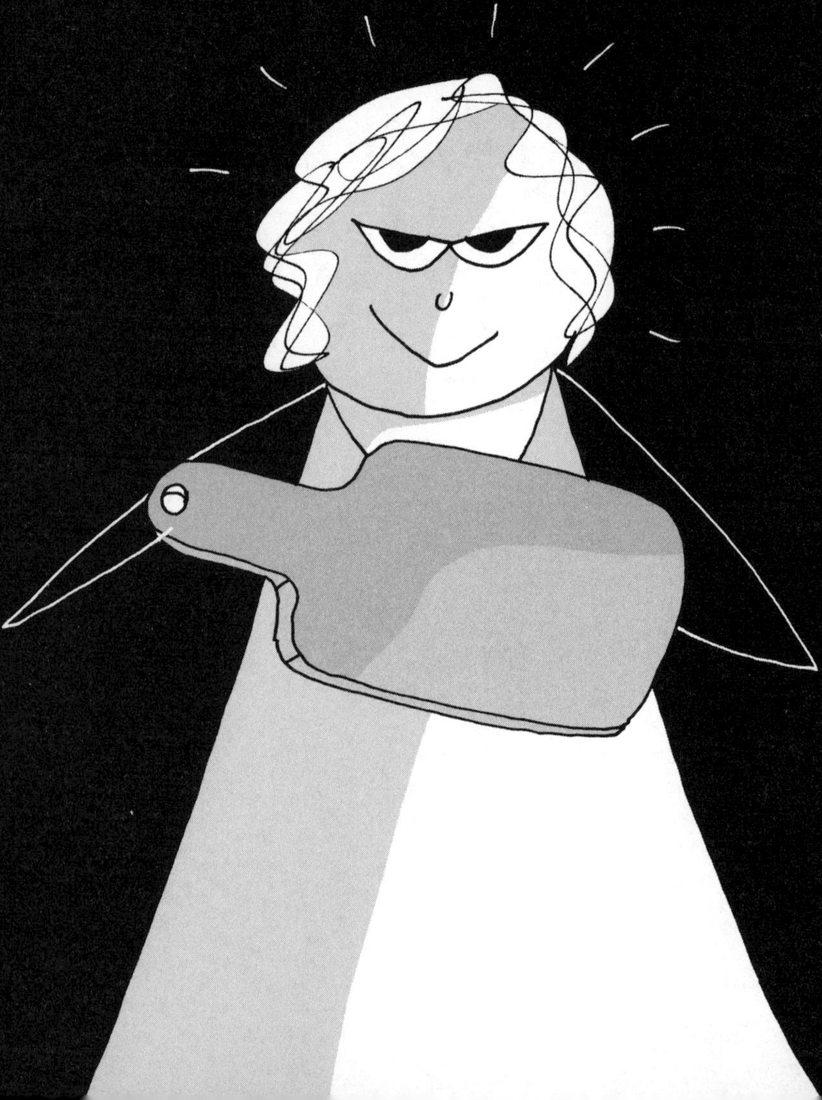

By this time Stephen Maysmith has
arrived. He puts Jo in handcuffs, and she
is gone.

CHAPTER THIRTEEN
A Bit Like Heaven, and a
Bit Like a Big Bang on the Head

But what about me? That's what you're thinking. Well . . .

That's what you *should* be thinking. The last you heard I was going flying over the door.

You should also be thinking about the pig!

One moment he's standing there eating his slops and thinking his evil piggy thoughts.

The next I've come flying in like a jet, and I've *head-butted* him.

The pig is knocked out cold.

Trouble is . . . I am also knocked out cold.

The pig and I are both lying side by side like a pair of sunbathers.

BUT...

Though my eyes are shut, in my head
I'm seeing A LOT . . .

I'm seeing Dad.

I'm seeing Dad on the last day I was
with him. We're in the park.

Then we're getting into his car.

But where are we going? What is about to
happen?

For a moment it feels as if I am about
to see it all again, and I will *know* what
happened to Dad, and I *need* that so much,
but then, also, at the same moment . . .

Back in the REAL world . . .

My mom is running toward me.

"Rory!" she screams, and my eyes are still shut, but I hear her fine.

"Rory!" she says again. She is really crying. "My beautiful boy! Oh my God! I love you so much! Oh, Rory . . . please come back! I would never shout at you again! I would give you ANYTHING!"

Hang on . . . ! *I cannot believe this!* I'm thinking: *I should keep my eyes shut. Any second my mom is going to say I can have her room and a new computer!*

My mom now REALLY CRIES.

"Roryyyyyyyy!" she sobs. "Oh God . . . You're such a *beautiful boy*!"

I open my eyes.

"Ah," I say, "you're not so bad yourself!"

And I smile.

And my mom can't help herself.

"RORY!" she shouts. **"What were you doing?"**

But I can't answer, because suddenly someone else is there.

It's the Cat. And I remember it was she who closed both eyes. It was when I said she'd called herself Cassidy Corrigan. *Why was that?*

I am just about to ask. But then she smiles.

And I try to get up (all cool) but I've really hurt my leg, so I fall back like a big toddler.

Then a third person appears.

It's Stephen Maysmith. Suddenly he's looming over me.

"Young Man!" he booms. "Are you OK?"

"I told you I would help," I say. "And I did!"

"You did well," he says. "But in future you keep your nose out of police business. Do you *promise*?"

I am thinking: *I have just found out that I am a detective. Now I am going to find my dad, and there is NO WAY on earth that you will stop me.*

But I don't say that.

I just say: "I promise."

And as I do I shut

my eyes.

Then I open them again, because I
have just had an absolutely brilliant idea.

"But you will have to do something for
me in return!" I say.

"What?" says Maysmith.

And I tell him.

And I'm delighted to say . . . he agrees.

It all works out exactly as I planned.
Better, in fact.

CHAPTER FOURTEEN
The Trip Home

For a start the Cat and I are driven home
in the police car. (Maysmith stops on the
way. I don't find out why till later.)

Then ...

When we arrive home, EVERYONE
is there. Cassidy's mom is there.
My mom is there. (She's already back!)
Wilkins is there.

The whole block is there, as we arrive.
And you can tell that the story of what's
just happened has already spread,
because as the Cat and I step out of the
car everyone claps.

Stephen Maysmith opens the back door as if he's opening it for a king and queen.

My leg is now hurting badly, but Cassidy helps me out.

I have to put my arm around her waist, but I find that I actually don't mind that at all.

First
Wilkins
comes
running
over (he is
so relieved
I got away
from that pig),

and so for a moment I am in *pure doggy
love heaven*.

And it gets even better, because just
then . . . Corner Boy appears.

"Rory!" he screams. "I don't believe it!
You were right! It *was* tetrodotoxin. The
hospital called. They've got my dad, and
he's going to be all right!"

"But," I call, "what about Mike Tyson?"

"Oh," says Corner Boy. "That's the best part."

"WHAT?" I shout.

"Mike Tyson," shouts Corner Boy, "has *just had a baby*!"

"WHAT?!!" I shout.

"Oh yes!" says Corner Boy. "It turns out Mike Tyson was *pregnant* (and that was why he ate so much) and now he's had a baby!"

"And," I say, "is he OK?"

"Oh yes!" Corner Boy assures me. He nods his head.

"Mike Tyson and his baby," he says, "they're doing fine!"

I laugh because I'm so happy. Then it gets even better. Because . . .

Only then does my brother's evil face appear at the door. And right at that very moment Stephen Maysmith, the police detective, turns to me.

"Rory Branagan," he says, "you have been a true detective today!"

He literally says those very words, and I just beam my face off.

"Two dangerous people were caught," Maysmith continues. "We could not have done it without your help."

Maysmith swivels to my brother:

"So you, YOUNG MAN," he shouts, "have to give him your complete collection of trading cards from the years 2010 to 2018!"

It is *so* fantastic!

"And on behalf of the police," he says, turning to me with a big warm smile, "I would like to give you these three packs of trading cards."

And when he gives them to me he says, **"Well done!"**

I go to my house. As I reach the front door, I see there's someone waiting for me, by her front door. Cassidy.

"*Deadly Branagan!*" she says. "What the *heck* happened there?"

"Well," I tell her, "I'd say Guinea Pig was poisoned by my Auntie Jo, on the orders of Thompson. She then tried to poison Maysmith to stop him getting her. Jo and Eyebrow then tried to run away: we took them down."

She gives me the biggest smile I've ever seen.

"I'd say that covers it!" she says. "Well done, Mr. Detective! You did well!"

"You did well yourself!" I tell her.

And I want her to say more but then she goes inside.

I don't actually mind. I'm suddenly feeling like I've been through a lot. I am thinking I probably need a moment to myself. I need to be in the tree house.

CHAPTER FIFTEEN
In the Tree House

It's not easy to climb up there. (I swear my leg could actually be broken.)

But it's worth it.

I have forgotten
my flashlight,
but the moon is
now shining so
brightly it
doesn't matter.

I open the trading cards, and I cannot believe it, because the first card is actually Dele Alli. I rip open the front of the pack and I see Dele Alli's smirking face grinning at me in the moonlight like a goblin, and even he seems to be saying, "Well done, Rory!"

I settle back against the tree.

And just then I realize I have
something in my pocket, which I have
actually been carrying since this whole
adventure started . . .

It's the letter that I found by the front
door.

I open it up and—to my absolute
astonishment—I see it's from Dad.

It says . . .

Rory,

I know it was your birthday last week but I couldn't get to a mailbox just then. So I am doing it now. I want you to know that I am fine. In fact, I'm in the place where I was happiest, and I want you to know that on your birthday I thought of you for every single second, because you are a boy in a million, Rory, and I love you to the moon and back.

Dad

PS. By the way you probably should destroy this letter now. And don't mention it to anyone.

I read the letter. Then I just stare at it.

For a moment it's like when I realized
Jo was the poisoner. I cannot move I am
so shocked.

And then I feel a bit dizzy as if I've
rolled downhill.

But then—of course—I start to feel very, very *pleased* and *excited*, because I now know for the first time in seven years that my dad is alive! And then—of course—I am more excited still, because now some very *detective-y questions* start LEAPING like dolphins into my head.

I am thinking . . .

Why should I not say anything about the letter to anyone?

And I am thinking . . .

Is it because it contains CLUES as to where Dad is?

And then I am thinking . . .

YES, IT MOST DEFINITELY DOES!

And then I am thinking . . .

And I am going to follow those clues and I am going to FIND HIM!

Because I am *Rory Branagan*, and I am *actually* a detective!!

And then I just lie back.

And I think of all the things that *have* happened, and I think of all the things that are *going* to happen.

And I just smile.

The End

The adventures
continue in Book 2!
*RORY BRANAGAN,
DETECTIVE:
THE DOG SQUAD*

My brother's

big head

appears.

"There is someone to see you!" he says.

"Who is it?" I ask.

But my brother just goes. No matter.
You don't have to be a genius to *detect*
who's coming. I can hear the Cat *singing*
as she climbs the stairs.

"*Dun dun der-dun der-DUN*," she sings. And then she *springs* through the door.

"Hello, DEADLY!" she says. (That's what she calls me!)

"Hello, Cat!" I say. (That's what I call her!)

I am so pleased to see her.

"So will we go out," she says, "so we can beat up baddies, and *solve mysteries*?"

"Er, no . . . ," I tell her, "because of my leg."

"Ah, I wouldn't worry about a little thing like that!" she says. "I have made something to help."

"What?"

"Jump aboard!" she says.

She then piggybacks me down the stairs,

making clip-clop noises, as if she were my horse.

"Behold," she says. "Your *chariot*!"

It's a trash can.

"I am NOT going in there!" I say.

"I have *cleaned* it," she says, "*and* I have put in cushions, and I have something very *detective-y* to show you."

She winks.

So that gets me curious.

"Stand back!" I say. *"I will mount the chariot!"* And I get into the can.

"Advance!" I shout, and we set off up the street (fast).

But as we set off I see the weirdest dog I have ever seen. He has a very long back, and a *long* face, but *tiny* legs, so he looks like a furry crocodile. I love all dogs, though, so I am *wanting* to go and pet him.

But Cassidy is in the mood to go fast.

"*Charge!*" she says, and *sprints* all the way to a store, where the thing she wants to show me turns out to be a magazine called *Real Detective*, but unfortunately we have no money, and I can't go into the store in my trash can . . .

. . . so we read at the door. *Real Detective* is fantastic. We just open it and we see . . .

REAL DETECTIVE

SECRETS OF THE FAMOUS DETECTIVES

SHERLOCK HOLMES: Always notice EVERYTHING.

HERCULE POIROT: List *all* evidence, list *all* suspects.

REAL DETECTIVE

SECRETS OF THE FAMOUS DETECTIVES

Philip Marlowe:

Don't be afraid to fight.

I am *loving* this! I am wanting to read
the whole magazine. But . . . just then . . .

I (Rory Branagan, detective) notice

something *very* interesting . . .

Actually it
hits me in the
face, and I have
to pull it off,
and I see . . .

MISSING DOG
Bryan — greyhound

491

I look at the lamppost, where I see more notices about missing dogs.

MISSING!
Sir Bernard
Ingham

St. Bernard
Call 619 - 3681

LOST
Believed Stolen

Sue + Pam
Lost on Flann
O'Brien dr.

CALL 614 - 3964

lost dog!

Taken from
Dean Swift
Drive Call
902 - 6610

I cannot believe this. Someone is stealing dogs from Dean Swift Drive (which is my actual road) and straight away I am very angry, but very CURIOUS.

And just then I also notice that . . .

. . . at the other end of the block, someone is leading away the furry crocodile and you can tell he does not like it. For 0.2 seconds, I can see someone. They are wearing a black hoodie.

"Quick," I shout to Cassidy. "I think someone is stealing that dog right now!"

"*What?*" she says.

"TAKE ME BACK! TAKE ME BACK!"

I am shouting.

"All right!" says the Cat. "There is NO NEED TO SHOUT!"

But there definitely is a need to shout, because if someone is taking dogs there is a DANGER they *might take Wilkins Welkin*!!!

To be continued . . .